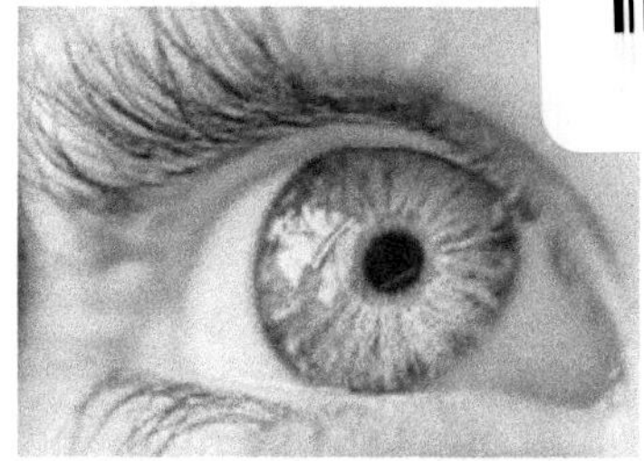

# The eyes of a stranger

## In a Starbucks – Sydney – Jan 2020

John is playing with his gold-plated Mont-Blanc while checking his mobile phone. His americano coffee is almost at room temperature now, but still untouched. He is half expecting a last-minute cancellation of this long-awaited meeting.

“Emily should already be here. She used to be very punctual. Right, but it was more than twenty years ago. Now, what do I know about her?”

His phone rings. Paul, his friend from Hong-Kong, is on the line.

- Hi, John. Is this a good time to talk?

- Hi there. I’m waiting for Emily. In a coffee shop. And she is late.
- You did it! Impressive.
- Well, I didn’t do anything yet. She might never show up.
- Man of little faith!
- I’m now wondering if I did the right thing. Maybe I should have left the past where it belongs.
- Too late to second-guess your decision.
- Maybe not. I could leave and forget all about it.
- Right. It has been twenty years and you still have not forgotten. Unless you develop Alzheimer, I don’t see much hope in the “forgetting” department.
- Do you think that anybody else than us, doctors, would laugh at this?
- Probably not. But who cares?
- Anyway, I prefer to wait for her a while longer and see what happens. The waiting for Alzheimer’s alternative: not so appealing.
- See, your famous common sense has finally kicked in.
- Oh, God, I think I just spotted her.

- Great. I'll hang up now and keep my fingers crossed. I expect a full debrief no later than tomorrow.
- You got it. Cheers!

## At Princess Margaret hospital - Hong-Kong – One year earlier

After carefully parking his Mercedes at the doctor's carpark, John takes a deep breath. And another one. And another one. And it doesn't make him feel any better. He decides to ignore it and to get on with his day. A bunch of interns are surely already waiting for him. No time for self-pity or introspection.

He walks briskly into the surgery building of the hospital. Many people are already queuing for a consult. At first, John used to feel bad for them. He wanted to change the system. He wanted to make it better for his patients. Now, he barely sees them anymore.

Princess Margaret hospital is one of the biggest in Hong Kong. It's not located on the fancy Hong Kong Island side, but has nevertheless proven itself to be one of the best hospitals, especially when it comes to kidney and related research. 4000 staff, 1700 beds. The size of a factory. Its many buildings all share one characteristic: they are oldish and could use some re-painting, but its non-stop buzzling activity makes it impossible to take time aside for a cosmetic make-over.

John has been working there for almost twenty years and made his way to the few coveted top positions.

He smiles as he recalls this very special Sunday lunch with his parents. He had invited them to the Peninsula hotel where a one-star Michelin chef operated a very expensive and delicious dim sum restaurant called “Spring Moon”.

Even though John lived for many years in Australia, he always had a fondness for Cantonese cuisine. He could easily defend it as the best cuisine in the world and loved this long-lasting habit of going to a dim sum restaurant with his parents on Sundays to eat dumplings. He had made sure that among the various dishes on the menu, like the well-known baked barbecue pork puff, they would also find the famous Siu Mai, a delicious shrimp and pork dumpling. He had tried many restaurants in Sydney, but none managed to re-create this unique taste of Siu Mai.

As soon as the dishes had arrived, he had told them the big news. He was promoted as head of surgery. Lu, his dad, was smiling and looking genuinely happy. He stood up and held his son in his arms for a brief hug. And that was it. After that, it was a given that John would continue to succeed as well as to have the perfect family.

John must be the best at everything to make Lu proud and it is exhausting.

“I simply need a holiday. When was the last time I took some time off?”

John is briefly relived to find a plausible cause for his lack of energy. He is simply tired of the pressure he has in all areas of his life, be it at the hospital or at home.

“I’ll ask Lola to take care of it. She will plan something for us. She knows how to choose nice and expensive hotels. All will be well after a break.”

His smile fades as he visualises the holiday. His wife will be at the spa all day and Mary will be handed over to a baby-sitter instead of staying with him. Better for her, will say Lola. Isn’t it strange that she feels more comfortable at the thought of a stranger taking care of the baby than her own father? It will surely not be the family vacation that he first naively had in mind: “rest and re-connect” will not be in the agenda. No, instead he will have to find a golf course to keep himself occupied.

“Shouldn’t I be happy to have a pretty wife and a healthy child? And a good job? And a nice car?” His attempts at boosting his morale fail one after another. “Ok, if that’s what it is, if you want to feel like an ungrateful brat, just go and do your work. Distract yourself with your patients and your interns. That’s what you are good at. So just do it.” The voice in his head won’t stop chastising him. The only way against it, is indeed to drown himself into work. And that is an easy thing to do at Princess Margaret.

“It could be worse. I could have a job where I have not much to do all day.” A very small satisfaction indeed, but the only one he can find for now.

## On a hiking trail in Lantau island - Hong-Kong

- Are you sure this is the right path to Tong Fuk beach? asks John.

- I'm pretty sure that we can get there from this path. Google map is confirming it too. There is a path on the right. Just need to get there and find it, says Paul.
- But isn't it also the way to Lantau Peak? I really don't feel like hiking all the way up there. Not today anyway.
- It's only 934 meters.
- Yeah, exactly. I prefer the beach if you don't mind.
- It's only the second highest point in Hong Kong.
- I still prefer the beach.
- Fine, you are no fun at all these days. You know that, right?
- Yeah, whatever. Are you really hundred per cent sure that we should follow this path?
- No, I'm not and because you are in one of those moods, I will stick to the original plan and make sure we reach the beach on time for our picnic.

A week ago, John had made a major decision. He requested one day off. Even though he is only entitled to ten days annual leave per year, he is still unable to take them all and is frequently harassed by the human resource director of the hospital, who doesn't like to have to forfeit them without pay. Paul, his best friend, whose hobby is to discover the many trails of Hong Kong, offered him to go hiking.

They walk at a good pace on deserted trails in the middle of a forest. They enjoy the fact that contrary to weekends, they are mostly alone and can walk fast without having to slow down because of other hikers zigzagging on the narrow paths.

- You seem a bit off these days, says Paul once he is sure to be on the right trail.
- I know. My head is not where it should be. And nothing I do seems to change it.
- What's going on? Any issue with the wife? With the baby?
- The wife has a name.
- Yeah, sorry. I just… You know.
- I know. No problem with her, business as usual. Not much communication, just the basic daily life stuff.
- That's not new. Is it only bugging you now because of your baby girl?

- Not really. I'm not getting any younger and I wonder if I made the right choices.
- Are we talking about Emily again?
- Maybe. I wonder if I should have come back to Hong Kong at all. If listening to my dad was really the right thing to do.
- You did what you felt was right at the time. That's in the past. What matters is what you want now.
- What I want? The impossible: having a family, a loving wife, a nice job and a proud father.
- Indeed, that might be mission impossible.
- I should be able to accept the life I have. Simple enough, right? But…
- For now, don't you want to simply look at what is around us? It might not solve your life crisis, but it's worth enjoying.

What they have in front of them is far away from the usual picture most people have of Hong Kong. No buildings, no crowd and buzzing activity. Just peaceful vibes and green all around. The beach in front of them is deserted apart from a young boy running with his dog. They easily cross the road as there are only few cars or buses. Lantau island, the largest and greenest part of Hong Kong, had the smart idea to limit cars through a licence plate system only available to residents. It proves useful especially on weekends. It's like being transported to another time and place. And yet, in no time, they will be back to the MTR, to the rush hours, to the cars and buses on the streets, to the noisy and polluted city.

For now, they choose a picnic table sheltered from the sun by a tree. Even though it's technically still winter, the sun is already quite strong. They enjoy some simple food while watching the water and chatting.

Paul is the head of the paediatrics department at the same hospital. They share their admin issues and the complicated cases of patients that make them feel powerless. They share the ups and downs in the life of a doctor.

## At home - Hong-Kong

A few hours later, John is back home, feeling relaxed after his outing with Paul. For once, he will be able to feed his daughter and put her to bed. He is looking forward to this sacred time with her. More than he should, he gives it away for meetings or patients. Not today.

His family lives in a nice and spacious house in Tung Chung, not very far from the MTR. They have a little garden and a roof top, where he loves to go and chill with a book and coffee during his free time. As soon as their daughter will be old enough, they will choose a dog together. It will stay in the garden. That's his plan. He loves dogs, but of course Lola doesn't. He is hoping that, in the future, his daughter will side with him.

His parents live in Happy Valley, on Hong Kong Island. Besides the possibility of a bigger house, he also needed a bit of physical distance from them. Lola was not thrilled by this choice. She likes shopping and the distance to her favourite mall, IFC, often makes her grumpy. As they have hired two Filipino helpers to take care of the house and the baby, she still has ample time to go there and spend John's hard-earned money.

He is surprised to find the house very quiet. His wife is not at home, and neither is his daughter. He asks the helpers, who only know that she left with Mary in the middle of the afternoon.

A few hours later, Lola and the baby are finally back. John has called his wife repeatedly on her mobile phone with not much luck. He also tried leaving a few messages, but to no avail.

- Where have you been? asks John as soon as he sees her entering the house with Mary and a few shopping bags.
- Good evening to you too.
- Don't think you can teach me manners when you have not even read my messages or called me back.
- I thought you were working, so I didn't check my mobile phone.
- I was NOT working today. I told you yesterday.
- Oh, true. You were spending the day with your buddy, I remember now.
- Exactly and I was hoping to spend a few hours with my daughter.
- Oh really? That's rather unusual.
- What does it mean?
- Nothing. Anyway, now it's bedtime. You can bring her to bed if you want.

- Yes, I want. I will speak to you after that. Wait for me in the living room.
- Right, sir. Yes sir, says Lola while handing over the baby to John.
- It's not funny, Lola. We need to talk.

Half an hour later, John is back with Lola. His mood is as bad as it was before Mary's bedtime.

- You know that I have only limited free time and you just disappeared with her.
- I did not disappear. I was having an early dinner with my parents. They wanted to see their grand-daughter and as we live so far from the city…
- Not that again, please!
- Why not? It was your choice, not mine.
- That is not the topic. Next time I take a day off, I want you to make sure I will be able to spend time with my daughter. Is it understood?
- Do you hear the way you talk to me?

- It seems to be the only way. Now you know without a doubt what is expected of you.
- And what about what is expected of you?
- Oh, smart reply. What are you now? A four-year-old?
- What I mean, John, is that if you let me buy a new car, it would be easier for me to get back home on time, as you expect me to, despite the distance.
- But you already HAVE a car!
- Yes, an old Volvo. How does it make me look like when I go visit my parents? Like you don't earn enough money to buy me a nicer one?
- Your parents never even had a car so they should be happy that you have one! And a Volvo is a solid and reliable car if you get into a car accident.
- Oh please! Like I'm such a bad driver?
- No, it's not what I meant. But you never know what can happen on the road.
- I'm sure a Mercedes or a BMW does the job too.
- Not as well as a Volvo.

- Anyway, not the topic, as you like to say. My parents want to see that I made it and will never ever again lack money. It's important for their peace of mind. They deserve that at their old age.
- You made it? You mean I made it because last time I checked your contribution to the family finances is null. Or rather say negative if I include all your shopping.
- This is so mean, John. I take care of our house and of course of Mary. It's a full-time job even if I don't get a salary for it. Did you forget that?
- Right, with two full time helpers.
- Of course, that's what everyone else does.
- Your parents did not have helpers, as far as I know.
- No, they did not. We barely had enough money for food. Living like that is not for me.
- I know and you are most definitely not living like that with me. Besides your car's little whim, I don't think you can complain about money. I even provide monthly financial support to your parents if I should remind you.

Lola looks at him. She looks miserable and her bottom lip is quivering.

- Stop it. I know your games, don't start crying. It won't work with me.

John looks at Lola. She would make a great actress. In a few seconds, seeing that her tactic is not working, she changes gear.

- OK fine, what is wrong with you, John? It has been weeks now that you are being a pain in the neck. What is happening? Do you have a mistress?
- I wish I had.

He walks out of the living room and takes refuge into his small office. He slams the door and locks it. Now, all he wants is time to think and try to make sense of his growing frustration and his inability to be happy. He wants to sleep on his own with only silence surrounding him. He can't bear the idea of feeling Lola's body close to his.

“A separate bedroom, it might simply be what I need.” thinks John while knowing all too well that he is just kidding himself. It would not solve anything.

## Sunday Dim Sum - Hong-Kong

A few days later, John is getting dressed to meet his parents for their customary Sunday Dim Sum lunch. Lola is with Mary as their helpers have a day off on Sundays. He can hear her screaming and asking for Lilly, one of their helpers. Lola is trying her best, yet failing, to calm her down.

“Maybe she is feeling the tension between her mother and I?” wonders John.

Since their last fight, they barely talked to one another, and John has been sleeping on the sofa of his home office. Maybe Lola didn't notice it as he usually comes back late from work and leaves early in the morning. He elected the nearby Starbucks for his breakfast before heading to the hospital. Even though he feels tired because of the few hours of sleep he gets, he also feels more peaceful when not seeing or talking to his wife.

But today, there is no way he can avoid her presence. And even worse, he will have to play happy couple for his parents' benefit. He doesn't really want to be scolded by his dad for not being up to his standard as a husband and father.

- John? Are you ready to go? shouts Lola
- Yes, I am. Need help to bring Mary's stuff in the car?
- No, it's already there. But if you can carry your screaming daughter, I would appreciate. She is beyond difficult today.
- Yes, sure. Maybe she is missing her nanny's familiar face?
- What are you implying? That I'm not a familiar face? That I'm not a good mother?
- I did not imply anything.

- Oh really?
- Yes, really. How about we agree on a cease-fire for our Sunday lunch?
- Are you scared of what your father will tell you if he knows how you behaved in the past few days?
- How perceptive of you!
- You are not even denying it? That's a new low. Even for you.
- What do you mean?
- You never stand up to your dad, that's what I mean.
- You should be happy that I don't.

His dad has chosen, as every week, a restaurant close to his home in Happy Valley. It's a rather long drive, according to Hong Kong standard. John is almost certain that his dad does it on purpose. He enjoys imposing a weekly forty-five minutes-drive to his son, if all goes well on the roads, to punish him for choosing, against his loudly expressed opinion, to live in Tung Chung.

John, while driving, is thinking that he did not follow his dad's direction on that one. Lola was wrong earlier. He feels a little surge of pride for sticking to at least one of his decisions despite Lu's loud displeasure.

He is hoping to easily find a carpark, which is not a given, especially on Sundays. His dad is walking to the restaurant from home. He doesn't have to go through this trouble. But for once, luck is on his side. Just as he arrives in front of the restaurant, a perfect spot is waiting for him.

John helps Lola out of the car and carries a sound-asleep baby Mary into the restaurant. After screaming during most of the drive, she finally gave in.

- If that is not my favourite granddaughter! says Lu walking towards John, all eyes on Mary.
- Hello dad, hello ma, says John, who has become accustomed to being invisible to his dad.
- Good morning, echoes Lola with a large smile.
- Take a seat, my darling. You look exhausted, says Lu.
- I didn't sleep much. Your granddaughter was having a tantrum all night long.

- I knew you would be the perfect mother. Didn't I always say it? says Lu turning to his wife who silently nods, as usual.
- And the perfect wife, you forgot that one, adds John.
- Yes, the perfect wife too. I sense some irony there.
- Of course not, dad, says John, already regretting his uncontrolled outburst.

"So much for a peaceful lunch if you can't keep your tongue under control." thinks John.

- Do you remember how long it took us to find Lola? It was not easy. But we are all very well rewarded, aren't we, my dear? says Lu.
- You are so kind, Lu. I'm far from perfect, but I'm glad you see me that way.
- What about you, John? Do you realize how lucky you are?
- Yes, of course I do.
- Good. I prefer to see you in this mindset, my son. By the way, how are things at the hospital?
- Everything's fine, thanks.

- Don’t you think that it would be time to open your private practice and make real money?
- I love my job as it is. I already told you. And we have enough money for now.
- It’s not a question of loving it or not. It’s a question of making money and being able to afford, at last, a nice apartment on the island, for instance. And later on, expensive schools for Mary.
- Oh, an apartment on the island would be great, says Lola.
- See, your wife – thanks, my darling – agrees with me. You need to behave like a father and a husband. You have responsibilities on your shoulders.
- How can I ever forget that I have indeed?
- Stop being sarcastic and listen to your dad for a change. Lola would need a new car. You would need to live on the island. And it seems that you can’t afford it.
- I like living in Tung Chung.
- Not that again, please. This is ridiculous and you know it. Why are you so stubborn? Why don’t you listen to me for once?
- For once? But I always listen to you, dad.

- No, you don't. Ok, you let me choose your wife. It turned out great.
- This is too much, really, Lu, says Lola while blushing.
- No, no, it's not, my dear.
- Yeah, she is right, it's too much. Let us be, dad.
- So why not letting me choose your living place and let me guide you to make the right professional choices?
- Dad, can we take that up some other time? I would really like to focus on the food and have some easy talk. It's Sunday after all.
- Ok, I know how much you love your dim sum. But I will not let this go.
- Oh, I have no doubt.
- Let's talk about it next week. I'll come over to your awful hospital. We need a serious discussion, my son.

John is happy to have a few days respite before his dad is on his back again. He feels frustrated to be told what to do. He has been an obedient son so far, but will this ever end? Can't his dad let him live his life with minimum interference? It's not like he is irresponsible and needs guidance. But it seems that in his dad's eyes, he is still this helpless teenager who can't decide anything on his own. Daddy always knows better. John starts to envy the western culture where parents are not too involved in their kid's life passed a certain age. Even more true when those kids are over forty years old!

He wonders how he will behave with Mary. Will he let her make her own decisions and mistakes? Or will he feel the irrepressible urge to guide her through life step by step? He sincerely hopes that he will find it in him to only offer his support and guidance when she will ask for it. To trust that the education he will have provided her through her childhood, will be enough to show her the right path in her adulthood.

For now, he needs to find a way to regain some freedom from his dad. Then he would like to go back to the "no emotion – no feeling" life he had managed for himself until recently. Else something major will have to change and he doesn't like the idea of it and the turmoil it could create for everyone.

## At Princess Margaret hospital - Hong-Kong – March 19

John arrives early at the hospital.

He is on to long hours, no days off and almost no conversation with his wife. The only major change is that his dad stopped interfering with his life. At least for now.

After the dim sum lunch, Lu had come to see him for a coffee at the hospital. He told him one more time to quit his job and start his own practice. He would help by investing in it. Against all odds, John simply asked him to mind his own business. His dad was so astonished that he did not even try to argue and simply left the coffee shop. John is still amazed that he could pull it off. He must admit that it felt good. He was also convinced that he saw a glimpse of smile on his dad's face. Or maybe he was dreaming it. But in any case, he is proud of himself. From that moment on, Lu stopped asking questions and providing directions. He apparently decided to enjoy the little time he could spend with John and Mary. That was unexpected. John had decided not to second guess his dad's strange behaviour and instead to simply enjoy it.

For now, John is waiting for one of his interns to come back with some additional reports on a difficult case that they have been working on since morning. Wanting to take some exercise, he decides to go to the common ward to meet him. As he reaches the female ward, he remembers that he forgot to look at the name of the patient. He rarely pays any attention to their names. They usually name them by their disease. As they seldom talk to patients, it's easier that way. But today this overlook will make it more complicated to find his intern.

He decides to wait at the nurse station, which is buzzing with the usual morning activity. He observes with detachment what's going on. He blocks the various sounds of human misery and the smell of elderlies, whose diapers have not yet been changed.

Breakfast, various versions of congees, is being served. The lucky ones even have a small box of orange juice carefully warmed to follow the diktat of Chinese medicine: no cold beverages.

He sees the back of a blond woman who is walking slowly towards one of the doctors. She carries her IV bag around, which seems to serve as her walking stick.

"Another one of those Chinese ladies thinking that they can die their hair blond and look like a westerner." he thinks with mild amusement. The colour looks different than what it usually looks like on Asian hair. He continues looking at the back of the woman who is now gently tapping on the shoulder of a young doctor who turns and asks her what she wants. He is close enough to hear her voice. "Definitely an overseas Chinese… I wonder what she is doing in this hospital."

- I'm sorry, I thought you were my doctor, my apologies, she says while looking at his shoes.

She turns around, obviously looking for another pair of familiar shoes that may belong to her doctor this time. John opens his mouth as he discovers that she is not an overseas Chinese, but a westerner. It probably explains why she obviously recognizes her doctor through his shoes. To her defence, he thinks, we all dress the same and wear a mask, which decreases drastically the possibilities to easily differentiate us.

He is so taken aback that he keeps staring at her. Public hospitals are for local people without health insurance or with a lousy one. Westerners usually qualify for fancy private hospitals with a private or semi-private room. What is that woman doing in the middle of a common ward? As he continues looking at her in bewilderment, she turns towards him and briefly looks at him and his shoes before moving on to another potential candidate.

And just like that, just when he finally felt better, just when he thought he had regained control over his life and happiness, everything collapses again. The sight of her blue eyes feels like sticking his fingers in an outlet and receiving the expected electrical shock. He has difficulty breathing. One of the nurses recognizes him and sees that he is not feeling well. She discreetly approaches a chair and runs off to her duty. She doesn't want to get in trouble with the boss. His legs are wobbling. He feels weak. He sits down and closes his eyes. He doesn't want to see those eyes again. Ever. Twenty years that he left Sydney and Emily. He thought that this workplace would always be his safe place. But even there, he is haunted by her and the choice that he made so long ago.

Will it ever end? Will he ever forget her? Will he ever be happy with the life he built for himself? Shouldn't he be content with all what he has? His dad knows better than him what is good for him. That's why he left Sydney. Could it be that he was wrong?

That he will never find happiness. His head is spinning. He feels like he is drowning.

Nobody can help him out of it. Getting cured is way beyond the reach of the doctors around him. Getting cured might mean leaving Hong Kong and his family. Getting cured might mean seeing Emily again. The cure is beyond impossible.

## A walk on Bowen road - Hong-Kong

After a few minutes, he recovers his strength. He gets on with the urgent medical case he was dealing with. As soon as they have established a plan for the patient, he calls his assistant. He tells her that he will take the rest of the day off as he might be coming down with a flu or something. He must give a reasonable explanation. He is very seldom on leave, let alone a sick leave. As a few nurses saw his “moment of weakness”, as he calls it, it’s easy to put it on a sudden virus attack. In any case, he doesn’t really have another easy explanation to offer. He is only sure of one thing: he needs time to think and sort through his thoughts and emotions.

He decides to go to the island and walk along Bowen Road. He doesn’t want an isolated hike. What if he suddenly feels the same weakness as earlier? He knows it’s not a rational thought. Nevertheless, he is scared. He wants to feel the city close by and Bowen Road offers just that. Just above Wanchai, on Hong Kong Island, it’s a four-kilometres trail overseeing the city and very popular with joggers and dogs’ owners. It’s mostly a no car area. It’s green as it’s carved out into the side of a hill. It’s quiet enough without the feeling of being in the middle of nowhere that most hiking trails generally offer, especially on weekdays.

Finally, it's very easily accessible from the MTR after just a short but steep twenty minutes-walk.

He arrives on Bowen Road all sweaty. Even though summertime has not started yet, it's already getting warmer. The high humidity level doesn't help. He slows down his pace and starts to re-live the recent encounter. A very active monologue starts in his head.

"I really can't keep going on like that anymore. It will even affect my work if I don't react. I need a change. I feel miserable. Is it the image of a father I want to give to Mary? My wife doesn't have the life she is dreaming of. I'm not happy and will never be if I stay with her. Everyone will be miserable. Only dad is satisfied. I did what he asked. Well, almost. He still wishes I'd have my own practice. He wants me to be as successful as him. To have always more financial assets. And what about me? What do I want? Nobody cares. I didn't even care myself to be fair. And who better than me, can take care of my needs? And now what? What should I do? It's all good to feel miserable. I don't want to play the victim role. It's not me. It will never be me. Maybe not, but you seem to behave just like a victim. You complain and you complain some more, and nothing changes. Ok, fine, things are about to change. I will finally do what I want, no matter the consequences. I will divorce my wife and move back to Australia. Maybe I could start my own practice over there. At least, this part will make my dad happy. I can be successful, I'd like that. I can do that. Yes, I must try it. I know it may not be ideal and easy, but it's my choice. It's what I believe would be best for me. And my daughter. She can come for holidays to visit me and I'm sure it would be a much better environment than Hong Kong for her. So that's it then. I have made up my mind. Let's try and make it happen now."

As he says the word in his head, he is also aware that having a fantasy about his future life is much simpler than implementing it. He will have to fight his dad and his wife to get there. And one sure thing is: they will not make it easy for him. Will he be strong enough to go through with it? Will he find a strong enough motivation to fight for his dream?

There is one last question coming back over and over again: will he be able to decide for himself against his dad? Even though he does resent the constant involvement of Lu in his life, part of him must reluctantly admit that it also gave him some re-assurance. He felt, in a way, comfortable not having to make his own decisions. His dad always seemed to know better. John had a tendency to procrastinate and to endlessly wonder which option would be optimal. In the end, he was rarely able to come to a decision. Lu's directions were putting an end to his misery. And he could even blame him if the result was not as expected. If he decides to take the steering wheel away from Lu, he will only be able to blame himself. John hesitates, terrified.

"Maybe I should simply take a mistress to distract myself. Or should I leave things simply as they are? Count my blessings and that's it." he wonders.

And what about Emily? If he is honest with himself, part of the plan is also to see her again. What if she forgot him? What if he can't find her? What is she changed so much that he can't reconnect with the woman he used to love? What if…? So many questions for which he has no answers.

On his way back, he decides to take it easy and daydream about life in Sydney. He needs some positive images and happy thoughts. The rest can wait. He can decide later. He finds it strangely soothing to walk while building an imaginary happy life where all falls into place easily.

**At Lu's house - Hong-Kong – April 19**

After his dreamy walk on Bowen Road, John had decided to take it easy, to see if he would still feel strongly about a drastic life change after a few weeks. He reverted to his life and carefully avoided the ward where the western woman was staying. He took an interest in her case so that he could monitor any risk of an encounter. In short, he was wishing her a speedy recovery.

He felt like his usual place of comfort- work- had become like a potential mine field. He could not wander around freely as he used to. He had to choose his routes carefully. He avoided any patient visits with his interns. He was monitoring everything remotely on the account of a surge of work that did not let him much time to handle ward visits. In any case, they were most often not even talking to the patients, but just talking about the patients. As such he decided that the interns would bring the patient files to his office for a review twice a week. His interns were quite surprised, but also annoyed. It meant more work for them and potential mistakes while placing the files back to their respective owners. John told them that it would be a trial run for about two weeks, after which they would evaluate the new method and decide to keep it or not. He was pretty sure that within two weeks, the disturbing western female would be safely back home.

After work, he heads to his dad's house for a light dinner. He also needs to pick up a few books that his dad bought for him. Around 7pm, he is finally free to leave and arrives shortly before 8pm at his dad's house. It's a large duplex in the back of a quiet alley in Happy Valley. Lu has bought this place many years ago and gradually did some renovations and improvements. There is also a private rooftop that his mum took over to fulfil her passion: gardening. She is mostly growing some fruits as well as some thyme, rosemary, basil, mint and parsley which she uses for cooking.

- Glad you could make it for dinner, even though it's already late.
- Sorry about that, dad. I know that you enjoy early dinners, but it's the best I could do. It was quite busy at the hospital.
- It's fine, don't worry about that. How are things at work?
- As usual. Too many patients, not enough doctors and nurses.

- I know, I know. But don't you think you contributed enough? Don't you think you could take it easy and have your own practice?
- Dad, we already discussed it.
- Yes, we did. Remember that I'm your dad, I just want what's best for you.
- Really? Don't you think that by now I'm old enough to know what's best for me?

John is surprised by his comment. He usually avoids conflicts, especially with his dad. Tonight, it's different. He badly wants a fight with Lu. He needs to prove a point. He needs to fight for his own desires.

- Not always. A parent often knows better for his kids. A parent is less clouded by irrational emotions.
- Oh yes, like when you chose a wife for me.
- What about her? She is dedicated to the family, takes good care of your daughter. What more could you want?
- Maybe I would want someone I love.
- Oh please, don't mention again that woman in Australia.

- And why not? I loved her. I wanted a life with her. Not with Lola.
- You had more common sense back then when you simply listened to me and came back to Hong Kong to marry within your own culture.
- Like you are one to know about marrying your own culture…
- Don't you dare talk about your mother. You know as well as I do that it's far from ideal. Yet, I sticked to my choices and stayed with your mum. I wanted you to do better, to benefit from my own mistakes.
- Was it such a mistake? You seem to have a happy life.
- It costed me my relationship with my own family, who never accepted her. And to be honest, she often doesn't understand me or our culture. It creates a divide between us.
- But she has been living with you for what? Almost fifty years?
- Yes, and almost always resenting the fact that I refused to live elsewhere. She wanted to go back to Europe. I didn't. I lived there for a short period of time and never felt at home. Furthermore, their Chinese food was horrible, and your mum never got the hang of cooking decent Chinese food either.

- If you had tried harder, it could have become better, easier, maybe even nicer than Hong Kong.
- And maybe it would have never felt like home. Her family never accepted me either. “The Chinese guy” as they called me. Even her friends made fun of me. All that pain for what? In the end, an unhappy marriage on the long run. One can never be happy without the support of the family. I saved you from that with Emily.
- You saved me from a life with the woman I loved. You and I are different. Mum and Emily are different. Times are not the same either. Mixed marriages are not frown upon anymore.
- I don’t see the point of this discussion. You have a wife and a child. Why thinking of what could have been? It will never be anymore. Choices have been made.
- Choices can be changed.
- Don’t tell me you are thinking of leaving your wife to go back to that woman?
- I don’t know. I’m just unhappy the way it is now. Something has got to change.

- Family matters. You made the right choice. Now suck it up. Have a mistress if you feel like it. It will distract you from that Australian woman. By the way, you don't even know how she has become, she might have turned into a fat and ugly one. Twenty years is a long time, especially for a woman. I have an idea: take a western mistress if you miss it so much.
- I don't want a mistress. I want a wife who loves me for who I'm. Not out of duty. Not for what I bring her financially.
- Stop dreaming. That doesn't exist. All women marry to get something. It's a transaction. You should know better!
- I don't believe that. I want a change of life. That's what it is, like it or not.

Lu's wife silently enters the room and is surprised to see them quarrelling.

- What's going on?
- Nothing. Your son is just talking nonsense. Is dinner ready?
- Yes, it is. I made some Italian dishes tonight.
- Why can't you learn to cook Chinese food? After so many years… I still have to eat European food. Really?

- But…
- Never mind, forget about it. You'll never get it anyway and it's probably too complicated for you to ever master the art of Chinese cooking.
- Dad! Stop it. This is really mean. Mum's cooking is excellent.
- Don't you dare mingle into my marriage and what I tell my wife!
- Well, you do mingle into my marriage without much hesitation, why can't I do the same?
- Enough. Both of you. Now come for dinner and stop this stupid argument.

Lu and John look at her in surprise. She is usually reluctant to interfere between father and son. But not today. Everything around John is changing. He wonders if it could it be a sign from the Universe. He smiles: "If only," comes to his mind while he walks slowly to the dining room where a nice smelling dish of Italian pasta with basil sauce is waiting for them. At least, he will try and honour his mum's cooking.

**Hospital visit - Hong-Kong**

John is having his morning coffee on the rooftop before going to work. His wife is still asleep and so is his daughter. He is happy to have some time alone. Since the heated discussion with his dad, a few days ago, he has been thinking a lot. What started as a provocation to Lu could turn into an action plan. He feels this would be the right thing to do it and yet he is still hesitating. It will create such a tsunami in the life of his wife, his parents, his daughter and of course his own that he doubts he can ever gather the courage to do it. But on the other hand, he doesn't want it to stay only a nice daydream.

He worries that not acting on it, will turn him into a frustrated, disillusioned middle-aged Chinese man. He worries that he will regret not trying, at least once, to be happy. He also worries that maybe it will not turn his life around as much as he believes. And then he would have ruined so much in the process and all for nothing. He has no guarantee that what he wants is indeed in Australia.

His mobile phone rings, interrupting his thought process. Before even looking at the screen, he knows that his mum's calling. He has set up different ringing tones for his friend Paul, his wife, his mum and his dad. It makes it easier for him to screen callers when he needs peace.

- Hi, mum. Everything's ok? I'm not used to your calls so early in the morning.
- Hi, John. No, something bad happened to your dad.
- What happened to dad?
- He had a sort of heart attack.
- A sort of? It's either a heart attack or it's not!
- I think it is. We rushed him through to the Queen's Mary and the doctors are with him right now.
- Why didn't you bring him up to my hospital? It would have been easier for me to check on him.
- It's too far. And I did not decide, it was suggested to me when the ambulance arrived.
- Ok, let me know as soon as you have more information. Do you need me to come over?

- Yes, of course I do. I'm scared, John. And I'm sure he got that thing because you argued with him over dinner. He was still very upset the day after.
- I made him have a heart attack. Are you serious?
- Yes, that's very possible. I saw it on internet. People get annoyed and upset and then they have a heart attack. It happens.
- Mum, I don't have the power to clog his arteries by having an argument with him. This is total non-sense.
- You can try and talk your way out of it, but it won't change my mind. It's your fault so you'd better come over and check on your dad. I don't understand the doctors. Come as soon as you can.
- Ok, mum, I'll be right with you.

John is surprised at his mum's change of attitude. He always had an easy but distant relationship with her. She silently took care of him and made sure he had all what he needed while he was growing up. She didn't do much in terms of discipline: that was Lu's job. He always pictured her as incapable of anger, at least directed to him. And now she almost yelled at him.

He quickly gulps the rest of his coffee, rushes to the bathroom, gets dressed and takes only a few minutes to call the hospital to inform them of his urgent leave due to his dad's condition. In the meantime, Lola has woken up and is sipping coffee, enjoying some quiet time before her daughter wakes up.

- Hi, John. All good? Already going to work?
- Hi, Lola. No, I'm not. Dad had a heart attack and mum is freaking out.
- Oh no! Do you want me to come with you?
- No need. I'll keep you posted.
- Well, I don't know what you told your dad last time you had dinner with him as I was not invited, but your mum told me he was very upset. It can't be a coincidence.
- Can you please just shut up and keep your medical theories to yourself? Heart attacks are not caused by a little heated discussion and dad has a history of cardiac problems and clogged arteries.
- Just saying… Surely did not help, but I'm no doctor.

- No, indeed you are not. I hear Mary crying. How about you go take care of her?

Without waiting for a reply, John takes his phone and wallet and leaves his home in a hurry. He doesn't feel very proud of himself for taking his anger and guilt on to his wife. He tries to rationalize his thoughts. "Yes, sure, stress is an aggravating factor, but then Lu was the CEO of a company. He is used to stress. Just a disagreement with me can't be that bad for his heart. Well, I don't know. But there is nothing that I can do to change it. I can just be there for them and that's all. Feeling guilty is not what they need right now."

With that in mind, he decides to do what he does best: action mode. He drives as fast as it is allowed and soon arrives at the hospital. He calls his mum to understand in what part of the building she is and rushes over there.

- Ah, you are finally here. What took you so long?
- Mum, I don't live close by. And there was quite a bit of traffic as usual in the morning.

- Well, if you would have listened to your dad, you'd be working and living on the island instead of that place in the middle of nowhere.
- Mum, do you really think it's the right time for that discussion? How's dad doing?
- I don't know. The doctor is with him right now, I think you should go and ask him. He will tell you everything as you are one of them.

Just as John is about to reply to his mum, a doctor comes out, obviously looking for them.

- Good morning. I'm Lu's son. I work at Princess Margaret hospital as head of internal medicine. How's my dad doing?
- Good morning. Well, he is not doing very well to be honest. He will need a lot of rest. You should avoid any stress in the coming days. Let's wait and see.
- Clear. What treatment did you give him?
- If you don't trust my ability to take care of your dad…
- No, not at all. Please forgive my son. He is still under shock. I'm sure you have done your best.

- No problem. Have a good day.

And before John has time to say anything else, he walks away to take care of other patients. John decides to go after him, but his mum holds his arm and shoots him an angry look.

- Don’t you think you should show him some trust and respect? Else he will not take proper care of your dad. Furthermore, he works for a better hospital than yours.
- This is not high school, mum. I wasn’t trying to pull rank, but to show him that I would understand whatever he would say. Anyway, I will directly check dad’s chart and that should provide all the answers I need. Then I can have a better idea of the situation.
- Ok, as long as he doesn’t see you…

John walks into the room where his dad is now asleep. He has many intravenous injections set up with various medicines. John quickly looks at the chart and the medicines given. He nods in silence and walks back to the corridor where his mum is anxiously waiting for him.

- I think he will be ok. You did well by calling the ambulance right away. It may have saved his life. For now, let him rest and see how he feels when he wakes up.
- Fine. Will you wait with me?

John looks nervously at his watch and mentally reviews all what he should have done this morning and the few meetings he had to attend. Then he sighs.

- Yes, of course, I will stay with you.

John starts looking at his smartphone and answering a few mails while his mum paces up and down waiting for Lu to wake up. Suddenly, they hear him groan lightly. His mum rushes over to him followed by John.

- How do you feel, my love?
- I've been better.
- Hi, dad. Don't worry, everything will be fine.
- How do you want me to stop worrying when you are ready to throw away the good life you have built up for yourself?

- Dad, please stop. I don't want to discuss it anymore. I'm here for you now. That's all-what matters.
- See, I told you! You made your dad worry so much that he had a heart attack. And what is this nonsense about your life change? Midlife crisis or what?
- Mum, please, I said I don't want to discuss it. Let's focus on dad and his speedy recovery.
- I wish you had given it a thought before scaring him and making him worry sick.

John doesn't want to put oil on the fire and decides to keep quiet. He walks out of the room to find the attending physician and discuss with him the next steps for his dad. That is chartered territory: it makes him feel in control and safe again. As he told his parents, the rest can wait. He is not ready to bear the weight of his father's death for stupid desire to change his life. All his preliminary plans and ideas can be forgotten for now. What matters is his dad.

"In a twisted way, Lu managed one more time to take control over my life. It feels like I can never get away from him."

## Virus attack - Hong-Kong – June 19

After a few weeks, Lu has made a full recovery. John spent as much time as possible with him and his mum. Lola, as usual, was very helpful and behaved as the perfect daughter in law, her favourite role. She cooked, she visited at the hospital, she visited at their home with Mary to make her father-in-law smile and relax. He had to hear many times their favourite mantra: Lola is the perfect daughter in law. He had little time to think about his own life. He had to deal with a relentless feeling of guilt for causing his dad's heart attack. His dreams became a distant priority.

John is at the hospital when his colleague, Bob, from infectious disease, rings his mobile phone.

- Hi, John. Is it a right time to talk?
- Hi, Bob, of course. It has been a long time. I usually see you around, but you seem to have disappeared those past few days.
- I know. You have not heard yet then?
- Heard what? Are you ok?
- This is not about me.
- What do you mean?
- I don't know if I should tell you. The hospital will organize a staff meeting soon.
- Now, I'm curious. And worried.

- You should be. We have a new virus. I have been working days and nights with my team on a few cases.
- If it's only a few cases, can't be that bad, is it?
- It can and it is. It's a completely new virus. We have no remedies available, and my few cases are in very critical condition.
- But have they infected anyone else?
- Not yet. They came straight from China. As they were sick, they directly checked in at the hospital. Apparently, many more people have the same disease over there.
- But we have not heard anything about it. Surely if it were so bad, we would have been informed. The world would have been informed.
- Sometimes, you can be very naïve, John.

A few hours later, John is invited to a meeting by the hospital board. All department heads are informed about this mystery virus which has elected Hong Kong as one of its new homes. His friend Bob is painting a grim picture of what could happen. They are all asked to make sure they have as many beds available as possible. All departments must be ready to shelter people with the mystery disease and need proper protective gears in place for their staff. He wonders if everyone is not being overly worried.

A few weeks later, John is not having the same opinion anymore. The virus has progressed very rapidly and contaminated hundreds of people already. Fear is spreading across the population. Strangely, the hospital is relatively quiet as many patients have postponed, whenever possible, their hospital visits by fear of catching the virus. Hospitals are now viewed as a dangerous place to go to.

While he is doing some paperwork, his dad calls him.

- Hi, dad. All ok with you?
- Hi, John. Yes, all good. Just wanted to see how things are at the hospital.
- Well, you probably watched the news, right?
- Yes, I did. Hence my call. Are you safe?
- Of course, I'm. I don't work at infectious disease floor. They are the most exposed.
- What do you make of it?

- It's hard to tell. The death rate is high so it may not spread that much.
- What do you mean?
- The more lethal a virus is, the least it spreads from one person to another.
- Because they die quickly before contaminating anyone else?
- Exactly, dad.
- Charming… so we should be happy that it's deadly, but hope it won't fall on us during the short time it may last.
- You got it.
- Don't know how it's supposed to make me feel.
- Well, you wanted my opinion. That's it. Not much we can do, but wait and hope for the curve to reach a plateau then decrease.
- On another topic, how are things with Lola?
- Not much change and we don't see each other a lot. She has quarantined me in the guest room by fear of the virus.
- That is a wise decision. She wants to protect Mary.
- And herself…
- That makes sense. Someone needs to take care of Mary.
- Yes, I guess.

- At least your mind is busy with something else than your eccentric new life plans.
- True!

John is thinking that the universe seems to conspire against him and his happiness. But he quickly stops this train of thought. People are suffering and dying. It can't be all about him right now. He knows that things will quiet down in a few weeks and then he will have time to decide. It will be his turn. Soon. He just needs to hang in there a bit longer and focus on his job. And on not catching the deadly virus.

It leads him to think about his wife behaviour with him during this virus crisis. While he understands why she is worried and wants to avoid taking any risk, he feels that she is not being supportive at all. Every day, a wider gap between them is taking place. She doesn't seem to notice it. Or maybe she doesn't care anymore. Maybe she believes he will always be there no matter what she does. Lu's blessing seems to give her a false sense of security. As if John would always want to please his dad. But will he always make that choice?

A beep from his mobile phone. A message from his wife. As if she had been listening to his thoughts. A mild annoyance gets over him even before reading it.

"Hi, John. Hope you are doing fine. I listened to the news and talked to my parents. We decided it's better for you to stay in a service apartment till the virus is under control for the safety of your daughter. I sent you the booking details by email. I have already dropped some clothes and various other stuff at the hotel for you. If you need something else, let me know."

John cannot believe that she is kicking him out of his own house without so much as a discussion. She doesn't even have the courage to call him to let him know. He is like a leper for his own family right now. Rage. Powerless. Unfair. He is not sure which one it is or maybe it is all of them together that he is feeling right now. He takes his phone and throws it against the wall. Luckily, it's a solid one that won't break that easily.

"Neither will I," thinks John still fuming. "She will pay for that. Soon."

## A tough decision - Hong-Kong – September 19

After two months of fear and long hours at the hospital, John feels that he can finally rest a bit. The number of infected patients has finally decreased. The ones who are still being infected don't end up in ICU or even at the hospital anymore. Furthermore, one eminent virologist from China has tested an old medicine used for parasites that seems to be working very well against this new virus. New disease, old remedy: an unlikely combination and yet the answer to the current crisis.

Those two months of intensive work and worry have left John totally exhausted, even more so as he was isolated in a sad, lifeless hotel room with no support from his family. After many hours of discussions, Lola has granted him access to his own house again. He was ready to use force as he couldn't bear the thought of yet another night in a hotel room. He is longing to see his daughter again. He is longing to be in his familiar surroundings. He is longing to be able to chill on the rooftop or simply prepare his meal or enjoy a nice coffee. But he is not longing to see his wife again. That is something that being away from her has made even clearer for him. Not that it was needed, in the first place.

After thinking about it for a few days, John decides that he is ready to talk to Lola. And he doesn't want to wait any longer. As soon as he is back from the hospital, he looks for his wife which he finds playing a game with their daughter.

- Hi, John! What's the rush? I was taking care of our daughter. Everything ok? says Lola while quickly checking that Mary is settled and safe.
- Sorry to interrupt, but we need to talk.
  John feels a little guilty about the interruption, but he decides to ignore it and focus on his objective.
- Sure. About? Did something came up at work again? The virus?
  She immediately looks worried and can't help but moving slightly away from John. He notices it and frows in annoyance.

- Not at all, everything is fine now that we have a cure. No need to be scared anymore.
- Good to hear. Is it your dad then? I saw him yesterday and he was doing perfectly fine.

The worried look is back. He is surprised to see how much she cares for his parents. Sometimes she cares even more than he does, which he finds somewhat embarrassing.

- Not my dad. It's…
- Oh no, your mum?
- Can you please let me finish a sentence?
- Sure. It's just that it always takes you ages to talk and I'm busy.
- Busy? Right… You have a very busy job, sorry I forgot, says John with a sneer.
- Don't make fun of me, will you? Taking care of our family is a busy job indeed.
- Never mind. I wanted to talk to you about us.
- Oh that! What about us? Everything is fine. What? Are you still upset about the few nights you spent in a hotel to protect your family?
- A few nights? I spent almost two months in that hotel!

- I knew it. You really know how to hold a grudge for nothing, don't you?
- For nothing? You got to be joking. I worked my ass off and didn't even have the comfort of going back to my family for a few hours of sleep before going back to the battlefield.
- See, it would not have changed much anyway as you only had a few hours free which you were spending sleeping! What's the big deal? I really don't get you sometimes.
- You can drop the "sometimes", you never get me. And that's exactly my point.
- Fine, John, I should have called you and made you feel more supported during that difficult time. I could have done better with you. Happy?
- Lola, I don't want to fight with you. I'm done with you.
- Ok, fine, you are right. Let's not waste our time. I'll go back and take care of Mary.
- Lola, I mean that our marriage is over. I want a divorce.
- What? You are totally out of your mind. You are still exhausted. Go to bed, I'll bring you a nice Chinese soup with some hot

water with ginger and everything will be better tomorrow morning.

- Lola, if it was that simple. I had lot of time to rest and think while you forced me to stay away from you. My decision is final. We just need to agree on the terms and the custody of Mary. I still want to be very involved with her, that goes without saying.
- You see, John, for me, things are simple. If you decide to get a divorce, your parents will side with me. I will do everything in my power so that you never see your daughter again. And don't even get me started on money. Be sure that I will make your life a living hell and will drain every penny out of your bank account. You will end up alone and ruined.
- Lola, you can't do that. It's ridiculous. Our daughter needs her dad.
- I can do that. I will do that. Our daughter is very happy without her dad. It's not like you spend a lot of time with her anyway. Little will change in her life: we will stay in this house that you will pay for. You will also maintain our living standards. She

will continue seeing her grandparents and will soon forget that you ever existed.

- Lola, you must be reasonable. I'm sure you are also miserable in this marriage. It will give you a chance to find someone else. Someone you deserve.
- Don't give me that bullshit, John. I don't want another man in my life. And I don't want to be a failure in the eyes of my parents and my friends. Marriage is forever. Like it or not. If you don't play by those rules, you will pay the price for it.
- Tell me something, Lola. Are you honestly happy with me?
- I don't ask myself this question. You provide for the family. You treat me well. I have a daughter who makes me happy and busy. Unlike you, I don't want the impossible. I see myself as a lucky woman. At least, till now.
- But don't you want a man who really loves you? Not someone who stays in a marriage because his parents expect it.
- Frankly? Not at all. I like you, but for me what matters most is my daughter, my parents, your parents, my friends and having a decent quality of life. I can live with a man who doesn't really love me as long as he takes care of me.

- We don't have anything in common. We don't like the same movies or hobbies. You don't understand anything about my job. And the list goes on.
- Is it what matters to you? I like your parents and I take care of them. I like our daughter and I take care of her. If you want me to watch a movie that I don't like, I will. I have all the time in the world to watch another one that I like when Mary is asleep. And even if I don't, it doesn't bother me.
- We can't talk about anything.
- We can talk about our family, our daughter.
- True, but is it enough? We can't talk about our feelings, our emotions. I feel so lonely in this marriage.
- Life is lonely, John. If you really need to share your feelings, talk to your friends. That's their role, not mine. We have a family business together. Would it be better if we were in love? I don't think so. Love fades away after a while, and it creates a whole bunch of problem. Instead, we can be rational and organize our life peacefully. No feelings involved. Respect and friendship is all what I ask and need.
- This is such a simple view of the world. Mine is totally different.

- Sometimes, simple is better.
- If it works for you.
- It does. And maybe you should try it as well instead of talking to me about this nonsense divorce. Be sure of one thing, my position will not change. I will do everything in my power to make your life miserable if you insist on a divorce.
- Why are you so evil?
- You would make my life miserable with a divorce. Why shouldn't I return the favour?

John can tell that he is losing the battle and that for now at least, there is nothing more he can do to shift Lola's perspective.

He steps into his daughter's room without another look at his wife. He looks at Mary, playing with her toys on the pink carpet of the bedroom. Suddenly, she spots him and gives him a large smile. He walks over and sweeps her in his arms. He kisses her and enjoys her baby smells. But Lola is already behind him, and the baby is now focusing on her mother. Lola takes Mary away from him and decides that it's time for the daily evening bath before going to bed. John realises how easy it would be for Lola to keep Mary to herself. He admits that he was indeed not present, waiting for her to get older, but also being fully occupied by his own work.

Now he doesn't have time anymore. Or does he? Maybe he should stay in this marriage a while longer. Maybe with time, he will be able to create a bond with Mary that will be impossible to break. Maybe his life is not as bad as it seems. Maybe he can have hope for a better tomorrow if he starts preparing for it instead of believing that all will fall into place without effort. He will have to fight Lola. He realises that he has greatly underestimated her apparent submissive behaviour. She knows exactly what she wants and is prepared to do anything to get it. This is a side of her that he never thought existed. He was expecting tears and weakness. How wrong of him! "Never underestimate your enemy." One more time, he forgot the favourite adage of his dad.

## Charlotte against the hospital - Hong-Kong – November 19

November has always been John’s favourite month in Hong Kong. He likes that the weather is cooling off at last and yet, it’s not yet Xmas with its many commercial advertisements. He always disliked Xmas, maybe because he doesn’t have the perfect family with whom to share it with.

Work is a bit slower than usual which gives him a bit more time for himself. Since his last discussion with Lola, nothing much has changed. They seemed to have had a tacit agreement to avoid any sensitive discussions anymore and to pretend that the infamous D word was never even evoked between them. John is not ready for a fight that may result in him losing more than only money. He can’t possibly give up his daughter. It might be selfish of him, but he loves his daughter very much, despite the little time he spends with her. And he is convinced that she needs him. But it goes beyond his love and her needs, he wants to show his dad how to be a good father. He wants to be the living proof that Lu could have done way better as a dad. He will raise Mary with love.  He won't impose on her whatever he thinks she should be doing. He will guide and support her. All what his dad could never even begin to think of as an alternative to his overbearing parenting style. Mary will become his personal revenge against his dad. She will showcase his victory against Lu.

Till it happens, he must find a way to cope with the lack of love and intimacy that his married life has become. He is thinking about what could offer a safe distraction to his misery when his assistant calls him.

- Sorry to bother you, boss. David is asking to see you urgently. He is with a patient.
- No problem, let them in. I am free now.

A few minutes later, David, one of his best interns, comes in with a woman following in steps. John looks at her and instantly recognises the western lady's eyes he briefly met a few months ago. For a minute, he feels out of breath and slightly dizzy.

Luckily, he is still sitting and doesn't feel well enough to stand up to greet them. He needs all he can get to recover from the surprise of seeing her again and all what she brings back for him. The woman looks at him and seems to be very aware of his uneasiness. She offers a kind smile in return which does nothing much to improve John's situation.

- Good morning. My name is Charlotte Brown.
- Nice to meet you, Mrs Brown.
- Call me Charlotte. And you are?
- This is Dr John Mao, our head of surgery, quickly offers David, mildly offended by the forward attitude of his patient.
- Nice to meet you, John.
- Dr Mao, insists David.
- It's fine, no worries. What can I do for you?

John turns towards David to have an explanation of the situation.

- Mrs Brown had a surgery at our hospital a few months ago and since then has been suffering from numbness in her leg. She believes something happened during the surgery and is requesting to watch the CCTV recording of it.

- Did we perform surgery on her leg?
- Not at all. She had a laparotomy to remove her appendicitis.
- Yes, which turned into a peritonitis because it took you guys forever to operate.
- But then, why are you complaining about your leg?
- My theory, John, is that whoever performed the surgery did put my leg into an odd position for an extended period, which led to some damages of the muscles and therefore the numbness and pain. Or worse. Who knows?
- Interesting theory. Did you consult with an orthopaedic surgeon?
- Yes, and she confirms that there was nothing wrong that could explain this. Just overworked muscles. As it started right after the surgery….
- But did you tell anyone about the numbness while you were still with us?
- No. I wanted to get the hell out of this place as fast as possible. I hated it.

John can't help but smiling at her very straightforward answer.

"Very typical of Gweilo." he thinks.

Gweilo, namely ghost, is the name given to all Caucasians by Cantonese people.

He had more time to look at her while she explained her predicament. She is probably in her late forties, very elegant, thin, tall, blond, blue eyes. She is wearing a short blue dress which makes her eyes stand out even more. He couldn't help but admiring her long legs while she walked into his office. She has a light tan. She looks like someone who frequently visits the gym. She seems pleasant enough even though her claim seems a little irrational to the scientist that John is.

David, visibly impatient to leave his embarrassing patient behind, adds:

- Boss, I'm sorry, but I've an urgent case to take care of. I have prepared the file of Mrs Brown for you and of course you can call me anytime if you need my help.
- No problem, go ahead.
- Thanks, boss. Talk to you later.

And without waiting for a reply, he leaves the office barely hiding a sigh of relief.

- Boss? Really? Do they all call you like that? Should I as well? asks Charlotte with a mischievous smile.
- Of course not, Mrs Brown, I'm not your boss, as far as I know.
- No, indeed. I take it that I can still call you John.
- Whatever makes you happy, Mrs Brown.
- Well, for now, calling me Charlotte will do just that.
- Well-noted, Charlotte. So back to your question. We can of course show you the recording, but it might be upsetting for you to watch.
- Yes, I thought of it as well, to be honest. I just don't know what to do as nobody seems to be able to help with this leg issue.
- Is it painful? Is it impairing your daily activity?
- I can't do as much sport as I used to do without feeling pain after a while. So yes, it's annoying. And I'm convinced that one of your boys did something wrong.
- My boys?
- Yes, your interns or doctors or whatever you call them.

- I see. So how do you want to proceed?
- How about we discuss it over dinner? I really can't stand hospitals. It makes me nervous. We could see what options I have and agree on a plan.

John is so taken aback, but her sudden proposal of dinner that he doesn't know what to think or say for a while. Then he wonders if that could lead to any more problems for the hospital, but he quickly concludes that if a dinner can make her and her claim go away, his boss would only be happy about it.

- That is most unusual, but if hospitals make you nervous, I wouldn't want to add to your current predicament.
- Great. Are you free tonight? Let's get it over with.
- I can be. Which place would suit you?
- We could go to a nice Indian restaurant in Tung Chung. That's quite close to my home and not too far from this hospital. I normally would be polite enough to offer you to go a Chinese restaurant, but I've had so many horrible Chinese meals during my stay here that I still can't bear the thought of eating Chinese

food again. Come to think of it, that's another complaint I could have towards this hospital.

- One complaint that I can't do much about. Let's go to your Indian place then. I certainly wouldn't want to suppress your appetite.

Charlotte reaches out for a mobile phone and after a short while finds what she was looking for.

- Here is the name and address. Should I text it to you?
- Sure, here is my number. See you tonight then.

John stands up to accompany Charlotte to the door. She offers her hand which he takes with a mix of pleasure and amusement. Charlotte has really made his day most interesting.

-

## Diner with Charlotte - Hong-Kong

John is starting to think that this dinner is not a good idea as the day unfolds. He has to admit that he is mildly intimidated by Charlotte. He doesn't feel at ease with her the way he used to feel comfortable with Emily. But on the other hand, it's just a stupid dinner to talk about her medical problem after her surgery. Not a date. Definitely, not a date. And on that note, he decides that he will get it over with and stop overthinking everything. To start with, he won't go back home to shower and dress up for her. Because that would be a date.

Even though he had trouble concentrating on the tasks at end, he finally managed to handle all the urgent paperwork and to be ready to leave so that he will arrive on time at the restaurant. She has chosen a very casual place. Is it another hint that it's not a date? John can't help wondering. He has not been into the dating game for so long that he feels like he has forgotten all its rules and may very well get it completely wrong.

He walks quietly to the place and tries to focus on his breathing and on emptying his mind. After entering the restaurant, he immediately spots her. She has chosen a remote table in the back of the restaurant. He walks towards her, with what he hopes portrays confidence.

She is deeply concentrating on the menu and doesn't see him approaching.

- Hi, Charlotte. Hope you didn't wait for me for too long.
- Hi, John. Not at all. I was just so hungry that I decided to come in a little early. And it always takes me ages to figure out what I want to eat.
- And did you find some dishes you would like?
- Yes, got a list of 5 or 6 which is surely too much for me…
- No problem, I trust you, let's just share.
- You are ok with that? You don't want me to show you what I selected first?
- I'm Chinese, I can eat pretty much anything!

- True. But I don't eat anything: I'm vegan.
- Right. So, no fish, no meat?
- No dairy, no cheese.
- Rice and green veggies then.
- Pretty much, yes. But don't worry, I found a nice selection.
- As I said, I trust you.
- Fine, let me order and we can have a chat.

Charlotte calls the waiter and gives him the list of dishes she selected. John looks at her and smiles. She is pretty and charming, but maybe a tad overconfident for his liking. He has forgotten the feel of being with a western woman. He used to find it quite normal. Now, he feels it's odd not to be in charge. He feels it's odd that she doesn't need him to talk to the waiter. He feels it's odd that he is the one intimidated and not her.

- Done, let's hope that they will bring the dishes quickly because I'm super hungry.
- I can try to distract you. Do you want to tell me more about your leg? And how I can help?

- That's not my idea of a distraction. I have another suggestion. Tell me about you. Wife? Kids?
- I'm married, yes. And I have a little girl.
- Nice. And happy with your wife?
- That is a very direct question to ask someone you barely know.
- I take it the answer is no. Am I right?
- Yes, you are. I'm separated. Or trying to be.
- It's quite simple: you are, or you are not separated? Trying to be is a weird concept. At least to me.
- It seems that you are a black and white kind of gal. I'm more into the shade of greys.
- Shades of grey? Interesting choice of words.
- I didn't mean to make a reference to… Well, you know the …
- The erotic book turned into a movie, you mean. That is quite a surprising thing to say to someone you barely know.
- I'm sorry if I offended you. I didn't mean to insinuate or start talking about…
- Sex? I know. Don't worry, I was just kidding.

The waiter arrives with the dishes and Charlotte welcomes him with a large smile and her full attention while he describes each dish.

- Perfect, let's start eating, shall we?
- Yes, please go first. I know you want to.
- Please move your plate closer and I will serve us both.
- Don't you want me to do it?
- Why? You think I won't be able to handle the spoon?
- No, no. I just wanted to be polite and offer my help.
- It's ok. You can relax with me, you know?
- Really? You seem very…
- Confident?
- Yes. And it's a little …
- Unsettling?
- Yes. And the fact that you always finish my sentence is…
- Strange? Annoying?

John looks at her and they burst out laughing. John finally starts to relax and to enjoy this most unusual evening. He starts talking to her about his family, his dad, his job. He suddenly can't stop talking. She is a stranger and therefore it somehow feels safe to share with her whatever has been on his mind for so long. She is a good listener despite what their first interaction could have indicated.

- You know what, John?
- No, what?
- You really need to start living for yourself and not to please you wife or your dad or whomever it is you feel the need to please.
- It's easy for you to say, you don't know my dad!
- It's not as easy as it seems, and I had to leave my country and come all the way to Hong Kong to finally feel free to do whatever I wanted. So, I get you. More than you think.
- I'm sorry, I shouldn't have said that. I don't know you and what your life has been about. And I talked way too much!
- I'm glad you did. You needed it. I don't. My life is not perfect, but is where I want it to be. For now. Except for this stupid leg that is.

- Yes, we forgot about this one. Should we talk about it so that I don't leave the restaurant feeling like an absolute selfish bastard?

Charlotte shares with him what happened, and John recommends her to go and see a colleague of him who should be able to solve this mystery pain and numbness. He believes that her leg was simply put into a bad position during the surgery and that she is now suffering from chronic muscle tension creating numbness. And not, as she seemed to imply, because one of the medical staff did something funny with her during the surgery. He was not sure she was joking or not. She was like a constant riddle to solve.

- I did enjoy this dinner much more than I expected, but I have to go back home. I need to be at the hospital very early tomorrow.
- We should do that again sometime. I live nearby. Easy. And just in case: I'm not looking for a relationship or anything. I love meeting new people. And I enjoy your company. Nothing more, nothing less.

- Thanks for clearing that up. Now let me take up the bill, it's not negotiable. Consider it as a compensation for your leg.
- Deal. Next time is on me.
- Next time. Yes. I'd like that very much.

## Check-up - Hong-Kong

The dinner with Charlotte has stirred many old memories for John. Mostly memories of Emily. It reminded him of a very different dynamic in the relationship, one that against all odds, against his upbringing and origin, he felt much more comfortable with. It required a bit of adjustment, like it did with Charlotte, but once he got used to it, he felt seen and heard for himself and not for what he could bring on a material or status level. In a way, more was expected of him: he had to show up and be present and engaged whereas with his wife, he only had to provide for her and make sure she had a comfortable and peaceful life. Suddenly he is longing to be with Emily again. The feeling submerges him in a way that almost scares him.

He is thinking about all that while taking his shower. He must hurry up as he is already late to go to the hospital. While he is drying himself up, he suddenly notices a funny looking stain on his leg. He wonders why he never saw it before. Immediately the professional in him takes over and he examines it as if he was a patient. And he doesn't like what he sees. Not one bit. For once he decides that his health would have to take precedence over his own patients and quickly calls a dermatologist, a good friend of him, who surely would find room for an appointment. He leaves a message: it's still early and his friend hasn't pick up the call. He tries to focus on getting ready despite a growing anxiety.

A few hours later, the assistant calls him back and tells him to come right away. Anthony will see him immediately. He leaves the hospital and rushes to the clinic.

As soon as he steps in, the assistant greets him with a smile. She obviously has been briefed and tells him that Anthony is just finishing off with a patient and will be with him within ten minutes.

John decides to sit down on the un-inviting little sofa in the corner of the room. He wants to take some time to breathe and calm down before facing his friend. He tries to rationalize and avoid imagining the worst before his friend has done a proper diagnosis. But deep inside, he knows he won't like the diagnosis. He just doesn't know how bad it will be. Just then, it occurs to him that he didn't even tell his wife about it. If he was married to Emily, for sure they would have talked about it. She would be sitting next to him and holding his hand. Her presence would comfort him. He would feel that nothing bad could happen to him. But for now, he is alone, and it feels like the worst could very well happen to him.

- Hi, John! Such a long time. I'd say I'm happy to see you, but your message really worried me.
- Hi, Anthony. Yes, sorry about that. And sorry for catching up with you only under this unpleasant circumstance.
- Don't worry about it. I get it. A job, a family: it's not easy to find time for anything else.
- Yes, and yet, it should not be an excuse to forget friends.
- Ok, so let me know what's up with you. Hopefully, it will be nothing!
- I wish. But…

John doesn't finish his sentence, but rolls up his trouser to mid knee to show the suspicious stain. The face of his friend tells him, even before he speaks, that he also doesn't like the look of it.

- Well, let's not get carried away. I need to do a biopsy. You know the drill. Even if it's cancerous, it doesn't seem to have spread anywhere else so it could be only benign.
- Ok.
- Let's do that. I will try and speed up the results and we should be able to have it by next week.
- OK.
- Try not to worry in the meantime.
- Yeah, that's also what I tell my patients before a diagnosis is confirmed. Not sure I can do that, but I'll try my best.
- I'm sorry, John. I know it's difficult and even more for us as we know what could happen and what it means. We can't even hide behind a certain level of ignorance.
- What can I say? This is what it is. Let's get it over with as fast as possible.
- Yes, I'll make sure of it. My assistant will call you the minute we have the report back and you can come see me to review it.

- Thanks, Anthony, much appreciated. I will reciprocate the favour anytime.
- Let's hope I will not have to ask you one anytime soon. It would be much more fun if you were a restaurant owner!

John leaves the office and decides to walk around the city to clear his head before going back to work. Strangely, the only person he feels like calling is Charlotte. Isn't it crazy? They barely know each other and yet, he feels that she would listen and understand. She would make him feel better. Maybe she would even find a funny way to look at things. But he doesn't dare calling her.

A week later, the assistant calls him to arrange an appointment. John has tried to live a normal life. He didn't tell anyone about the biopsy. He didn't want to make it real by discussing it with his wife or even Paul. He decided to try his best to forget about it until the results come back. And now is the time to face reality. Again. Alone.

John comes into the clinic. It feels like waiting for the jury to declare him guilty or not. Will it be a death sentence or freedom?

Anthony opens the door of his office to greet him.

- Hi, John. I'll go straight to the point as I believe you are not in a mood for some small talk.
- Hi, Anthony. Yes, please do.
- Well, it's overall good news. You have a cancerous cell, but it's only benign so we will be able to fully remove it today and you should be good to go after that. The only thing I would recommend is to avoid sun as much as possible from now on. And of course, we'll do some regular checks to make sure nothing else comes up.
- Are you sure? Isn't it going to spread? Skin cancer can be nasty.
- Yes, some can be. But you are a lucky bastard: yours is a very mild one. I promise that it will soon be over.
- Thank you, Anthony. I feel so relieved.

- No worries, let get this over with now and you can get on with your life as if nothing happened. Unless you want to wait for your wife before we do the procedure?
- No, thanks, she is not coming.
- Oh really? I get it, she must be busy.
- I didn't tell her anything.
- I see. Well, let's get going then.

## Recovery - Hong-Kong

Even though Anthony said that the skin cancer was only minor, he had recommended a few sessions with a psychologist. It became a standard practice after noticing how difficult it was to process the word cancer for most of his patients. Even when it was far from life threatening. He had seen a much easier acceptance after only a few sessions with the psychologist he was working closely with.

And that's how John finds himself in yet another waiting room. He has only accepted to do it after his friend heavily insisted. Even though he would have prescribed it to his patients if he believed it could help them, it never crossed his mind that it could apply to him one day. It makes him feel weak. What would his father say if he knew? He would not hear the end of it. Lu would surely make fun of him or look at him with even more disdain than usual. "Nobody should know about this, not even my wife." he decides.

After a few more minutes, an elegant middle-aged western woman walks towards him and greets him with a smile.

- Hi, John, I'm Ophelia, Anthony's friend. Well, we also work a lot together, I should add.

John never thought that he would be faced with yet another blue eyes Caucasian woman. It feels like a curse, or maybe a call from the universe, again. He can't really decide, but surely it feels like something he should face at some point. He can't keep going with weak legs, rapid breathing, a feeling of drowning every time his path crosses with one western lady with blue eyes. No, it definitely can't be right.

- John? Are you alright?
- Yes, sorry, Ophelia. Nice to meet you.
- Let's get into my office. Would you like a glass of water? Green tea maybe?
- Water will do, thanks.

John follows her and tries his best to focus on slowing down his breathing, on putting one foot after another in front of him until he reaches the inviting red chair, surrounded by comforting looking pillows. It seems silly, but it makes him feel safer. He sits with relief, exhausted by the swirl of emotions that has taken over him.

- Let's talk about that, John.
- About what?
- About how you feel right now as I can tell that a lot is going on and it seems I triggered it somehow. Tell me more.

John is surprised that a total stranger could pick up so easily on his inner storm, but after all, this is surely what she has been trained to do.

- It's just… your eyes.
- My eyes? Interesting. Who did they make you think of?
- Emily.
- That's good, John, you are doing very well. This is what this is all about. Think of it as unloading your emotions in a safe place so that it doesn't burden you anymore.
- Right.
- Emily. Who is she?
- My previous girlfriend, back in Australia. She has blue eyes, just like you. And these days any woman with blue eyes brings me this…. I don't know… flooding of emotions and it takes my breath away. But not in the right way.
- Not in the right way?
- Yes, makes me weak and I feel like an idiot.
- Your inner voice says, "I feel like an idiot," is that right, John?

- Not my inner voice, my dad. He would think I'm a total idiot and failure.
- Is that so? Do you feel like an idiot and failure, John?
- Honestly, I don't know. I can't keep up with what he wants me to be and at the same time, the more I try to do what he wants, the worst it makes me feel.
- And what is it that he wants you to be?
- He wants me to become even more successful and open up my own clinic and be happy with the wife he chose for me. Be the perfect husband, father and successful businessman.
- And what do you want to be, John?
- I like working in a public hospital. It makes me feel good helping people who can't afford expensive doctors. And I'm good at my job so they get the best. It feels like…I don't know, a calling.
- Maybe this is what being a doctor should always be: offering the best to patients, no matter what money they have or not, don't you think?
- Yes, I agree. But my dad doesn't agree.
- Ok, he doesn't agree. Why does it matter so much to you?

- Because as a son, it’s my duty to do what he wants me to do.
- Says who?
- I don’t know, society. The way it is done by everyone.
- Do you think that everyone follows their parents’ wishes to the letter?
- Actually, in Asia, mostly yes. But in Europe, no. Well, I don’t think they do. Not as much as us, in Asia.
- True. And what would happen if you don’t follow his wishes?
- He would be disappointed; he is already rather disappointed, so I don’t think he could take more.
- Did you ask him about that?
- No, I know. No need to talk about it.
- Ok, let’s put that aside for a minute. What would happen if he would become even more disappointed in your choices, but he sees you happier?
- Maybe he would not want to talk to me, or he would look at me in a way that says “son, you are such a disgrace.”
- And how would it make you feel if your choices brought you happiness?

- That he doesn't understand me, that he doesn't get me.
- Yes, and how could he possibly understand you?
- Maybe if we had a talk about what matters to me and why. And compare it with what matters to him and why?
- Yes, that's an excellent start, John. Now what would you want to be if all was possible? Just imagine, no barrier, no limitation.
- I would like to be a doctor in Australia. I love this country more than my own. I love the freedom. And I love Emily.
- Oh, Emily again.
- Yes, I would like to be with her. Leave my wife and be with her.
- That's excellent, John. We made real progress, you did very well. You really did.
- But we didn't talk about the… you know?
- Cancer? We will, John, we will. I hope that you'll stick around. There are lots of things in your life you need to adjust, so it seems. Cancer might not be your most pressing issue right now.
- I never thought I would say that, but yes, I would like to.

- Why does it surprise you so much?
- Oh, before it always seemed to me like a very selfish exercise.
- Talking to a psychologist?
- Yes. Feels like very self-centred.
- And it is. But not only. Knowing yourself better means more quality inter-actions with your loved ones, don't you think?
- I guess so.
- Fine, let's meet again next week if your busy schedule allows.
- Sure, thanks a lot, Ophelia.

John leaves her office feeling lighter than he had in months, maybe in years even. He knows what he needs to do. Without a doubt. And it feels good to have a future that looks like what he only dared dreaming of until now.

## Leaving - Hong-Kong – December 19

John decided to follow up with a few more sessions to help him see clearly what to do, but mostly to have someone in his corner while he was having difficult, yet needed, discussions with his dad and with his wife.

His dad, surprisingly, didn't try very hard to change his mind when he told him about his plans. He just said that he expected it for a while. He only tried to convince him not to leave Hong Kong for good because he wanted him to stay close by. He also told him not to hurt his wife as he genuinely liked her like a daughter. He didn't want John to be in a marriage with a Caucasian woman because he knew first-hand how difficult it was. He explained to John all that had been going on in his own marriage, at least at the beginning. He didn't want that for his son. But he also could tell that John was not happy and that Emily was still the one for him. John was stunned about his dad's change of attitude and at the same time felt stupid for not trusting that his dad would , in the end, show him some level of support. It made him feel confident that his dad would be behind his new life choice even though he didn't like its implications and was worried about him.

When it came to Lola, it was a whole different story and it costed him many sleepless nights either because they would fight for hours on end or because he would not be able to sleep, afraid to lose his daughter in the process. In the end, he promised her that the divorce settlement would leave her with more than enough money and that he would always support her financially as long as he could see his daughter regularly and have at least weekly video calls with her. He didn't bend and at some point,

Lola told him that she was ok with his proposal. It was not how she had envisioned her life, but she grew tired of fighting.

John is now just out from his boss' office having just finished his last difficult conversation: his resignation. His boss was disappointed, but had seen many of his staff fleeing Hong Kong in the past months. The handover to China had led many locals to find themselves another life in a freer western country.

This being done, he is heading to a coffee shop to meet up Paul. He wants to update him on the latest events. He has been quite busy in the past weeks, which didn't leave much room for a relaxed chat with his friend. They decided for a "talking walk," as they called it, on Bowen Road.

- Hi, Paul, so happy you could meet me. I feel I have been a bad friend. Didn't have much time for you recently.
- Hey, John. No worries. It seems I missed a few episodes. Tell me everything!
- Well, I'll make it short: I decided to leave Hong Kong and go back to Australia.
- At last!

- What? You don't even seem surprised.
- Well, I'm not surprised by your choice. You were always much happier in Australia and …
- Yes, Emily. I reached out to her. She replied. Briefly. That we should meet up when I'm in Sydney. She didn't want to talk to me or continue emailing. I guess she will only believe me when she sees me.
- Probably. And did you find a job?
- Yes, I found a position in the hospital I used to work at. Same as my position here. And I can start in a month.
- Wow. So fast, you did speed things up.
- I have no time to waste. This skin cancer did that to me. In the end, it was a good thing even if it seems rather strange to call a cancer a good thing.
- Indeed. What about Lola?
- She agreed to a divorce, we should get it finalised next week. I give her money. She gives me my daughter. In a nutshell.
- Yeah, that's how she operates. Not surprising of her.
- I don't mind. Money is not my main concern. I want to be happy. I feel like I have barely been living all those years.

Having a wife that I don't love and trying endlessly to please my dad.

- I'm really happy for you. I guess your dad fought against your decision, right?
- Not really. He wasn't happy about it, for sure. But in a way, he understood and knew he could not keep me in Hong Kong with Lola forever.
- No, really? Well, everything is working for the best in all areas of your life.
- Except one.
- Which one?
- I will lose my best friend.
- Of course not. We can always stay in touch. Furthermore, we talked about leaving Hong-Kong. You know that Anna always dreamed of living abroad. Australia seems like a good choice for both of us.
- Oh! That would be a dream come true!
- I'm just warning you: we may follow you and crash at your place one day while getting ourselves settled in.
- Nothing could make me happier.

- That I don't believe… I think someone else could make you happier.
- Yeah, Emily… I know. I'm so excited, but also scared to see her. What if she doesn't want me in her life? You know I don't expect that we will take it where we left it. I just hope we can at least be friends. I want her in my life, one way or the other.
- Just tell her that. Seems that honesty and transparency with your loved ones have worked well for you.
- It did. Good advice, thanks, Paul.

## In a Starbucks – Sydney – Jan 2020

After hanging up with Paul, John tries to take a deep breath and to steady his racing heart. He closes his eyes for a few seconds then looks at the woman who is walking towards him. She looks exactly like the Emily he remembers. He almost can't believe it. She suddenly stops, looks around her then spots John. And just there, he realizes that something is off. She is way younger than Emily could be, and she has dark brown eyes. John is confused.

- Hi. Are you John?
- Yes. And you are?
- I'm Emily's daughter, my name is Carrie.
- Carrie, where is Emily? She couldn't make it and sent you instead? Why?
- She didn't send me, well, not really.
- I don't understand.
- I don't know how to say this. I wanted to tell you face to face.
- Go ahead. She doesn't want to see me anymore, is that it? But why send you? This is strange.
- She died. Six months ago. She had a heart attack. She was very healthy. It took us all by surprise.
- Oh no. This can't be happening. No.
- I'm sorry, John. I kept her Facebook profile active because I like looking at her posts, but also to inform her close friends.

In a way, you are one of them. I was about to reach out to you when you got in touch.

- Oh my God. She can't be gone. You know, your mum is the love of my life.
- Well, no, I don't know. Neither did mum. She often talked about you. She wondered what you were doing and if you were happy.
- Really?
- Yes, because when you left her, you didn't only leave her. You also left me.
- What?
- She was about to tell you that she was pregnant when you told her about your decision to go back to Hong Kong as your dad had requested. You said he would never approve of her and that you couldn't deal with it. You simply had to obey. A huge load of bullshit if you want my opinion. Who could possibly listen to his dad when it comes to choosing a wife? Ridiculous.

- I know. I was young, I was naïve. In the end, I couldn't live with it and decided to come back to your mum, but I'm too late.
- What did you expect? Things change in twenty years.
- Yes. Can't get my head around the fact that you are my daughter.
- From a genetic standpoint, yes.
- But why would she do that? Why not letting me know about the baby?
- She decided to let you go because she didn't want you to be conflicted between your family and her. That's how much she loved you.
- Oh no. No. I can't possibly have abandoned you too.
- It's Ok, John. After you left, she met a very nice man. He knew mum was pregnant. He couldn't have children of his own. He loved mum and wanted more than anything else to be with her and be a dad. That's what he got, I guess I can say, thanks to you. He is a great dad and I love him more than…

- You could ever love me. Right? That's fair. I get it.
- Yes. I'm sorry, John. Plus, it would be very unfair to dad, who has always been there for me. Now, he needs me. Losing mum took a toll on him.
- I can't believe I didn't notice or guess anything. I can't believe I left and never checked on her. I can't believe I have such a beautiful daughter.
- Wherever she is, she is surely happy to know that you came back, that you didn't forget her.
- I never forgot her. Never. But I'm too late.
- Even if it's too late, I thought you would have wanted to know the truth.
- Of course, and I'm grateful that you had the courage to come and tell me everything. It would have been much easier to ignore and forget all about me.
- Yes, it would have. I was curious to see you, if I want to be honest. Dad pushed me to come. He didn't want me to have any regret for not doing it while I had a chance. Who knows when you are going to flee this country again?

- Your dad…
- Andrew. His name is Andrew.
- Andrew seems like a great guy. I don't know how I could ever thank him for what he did.
- There is no need to do that. He is my dad. That's what dads do for their daughters. DNA is not everything.
- Right, yes of course.
- Well, I told you all there is to know…
- And thanks again for that. I hope you will give me chance to spend time with you. I don't want to replace your dad or anything like that. Maybe you could consider a second dad. Or simply getting to know each other…
- I don't know. Maybe. I need to think about it.

They continue chatting for a while until Carrie sees her dad waving at her from the street. She waves back and smiles at him then turns to John, leaves him quickly her number and immediately stands up and go. John sees her walk towards Andrew who takes her in his arms then they walk together and disappear out of John's sight.

Just when he thought he had it all finally figured out, John finds himself in an unknown territory. Strangely, he has no regret for leaving his easy and comfortable life in Hong Kong behind. He only feels tired, sad, lonely and at the same time excited by the prospect to get to know his daughter.

"Can you really start-over at forty-five years old and manage to find peace and happiness?" he asks himself.

He is not sure he knows the answer. The only thing he knows is that he will try his best to rebuild a life, his life, the way he wants it with his daughters at the centre. Because right now, this is all-what matters.

He is ready to leave the coffee shop when his phone rings.

- John!
- Yes, Lola. What's up?
- John, you need to come back to Hong Kong at once.
- Why?

- Your mum has been diagnosed with liver cancer. She needs you by her side.
- Oh my God! She didn't seem ill at all before I left.
- She probably didn't want to say anything, you know your mum. She is always very discreet and doesn't want to upset your dad. Or maybe it's your departure who made her sick.
- Stop it, Lola, I will not take that crap from you.
- Sorry, John. It's just that it has been hard for all of us without you.
- It's an adjustment for everyone, trust me.

After gathering more information about what happened during the few weeks he has been away, he hangs up the phone and tries to gather his thoughts. This time, he will not make the same mistakes he did twenty years ago. He will take care of the ones he loves in Hong Kong and he will continue with his life here in Sydney. Travelling back and forth is the only solution for now. He will not give up his dreams. He will not abandon his newly found daughter, and neither will he abandon Mary or his parents. They will find a place in his life. One way or another. He will compromise, but he will not change his choice, no matter how hard it will be. With that newly found strength, he feels ready to face anything that will come his way.

-

www.ingramcontent.com/pod-product-compliance
Lightning Source LLC
LaVergne TN
LVHW050316160826
845677LV00014B/3429
* 9 7 9 8 3 6 2 2 9 0 7 5 7 *